Dear Parent:

Congratulations! Your child is taking the first steps on an exciting journey. The destination? Independent reading!

STEP INTO READING® will help your child get there. The program offers five steps to reading success. Each step includes fun stories and colorful art. There are also Step into Reading Sticker Books, Step into Reading Math Readers, Step into Reading Write-In Readers, Step into Reading Phonics Readers, and Step into Reading Phonics First Steps! Boxed Sets—a complete literacy program with something for every child.

Learning to Read, Step by Step!

Ready to Read   Preschool–Kindergarten
• **big type and easy words** • **rhyme and rhythm** • **picture clues**
For children who know the alphabet and are eager to begin reading.

Reading with Help   Preschool–Grade 1
• **basic vocabulary** • **short sentences** • **simple stories**
For children who recognize familiar words and sound out new words with help.

Reading on Your Own   Grades 1–3
• **engaging characters** • **easy-to-follow plots** • **popular topics**
For children who are ready to read on their own.

Reading Paragraphs   Grades 2–3
• **challenging vocabulary** • **short paragraphs** • **exciting stories**
For newly independent readers who read simple sentences with confidence.

Ready for Chapters   Grades 2–4
• **chapters** • **longer paragraphs** • **full-color art**
For children who want to take the plunge into chapter books but still like colorful pictures.

STEP INTO READING® is designed to give every child a successful reading experience. The grade levels are only guides. Children can progress through the steps at their own speed, developing confidence in their reading, no matter what their grade.

Remember, a lifetime love of reading starts with a single step!

Thomas the Tank Engine & Friends™

A BRITT ALLCROFT PRODUCTION

Based on The Railway Series by The Reverend W Awdry
© 2007 Gullane (Thomas) LLC
Thomas the Tank Engine & Friends and Thomas & Friends are trademarks
of Gullane (Thomas) Limited. Thomas the Tank Engine & Friends and Design
is Reg. U.S. Pat. & Tm. Off.

A HIT Entertainment Company

www.stepintoreading.com
www.thomasandfriends.com

Educators and librarians, for a variety of teaching tools, visit us at
www.randomhouse.com/teachers

Library of Congress Cataloging-in-Publication Data
Henry and the elephant / illustrated by Richard Courtney.
p. cm. — (Step into reading. A step 2 book) "Thomas the tank engine & friends."
Based on The railway series by the Rev. W. Awdry.
"A Britt Allcroft production."
SUMMARY: A runaway elephant blocks a tunnel and causes trouble for Henry and his friends.
ISBN: 978-0-375-83976-4 (trade) — ISBN: 978-0-375-93976-1 (lib. bdg.)
[1. Railroads—Trains—Fiction. 2. Elephants—Fiction.] I. Courtney, Richard, ill. II. Awdry, W.
III. Series: Step into reading. Step 2.
PZ7.H39741 2007   [E]—dc22   2006027007

Printed in the United States of America
10 9 8 7 6 5 4
First Edition

Henry and the Elephant

Based on *The Railway Series*
by the Rev. W. Awdry

Illustrated by Richard Courtney

Random House 🏠 New York

Thomas left the Yard.
He went to run
his own Branch Line.

Henry and Gordon

missed Thomas.

5

With Thomas gone,
there was more
work to do.
Henry and Gordon
were cross.

Henry grumbled
as he pushed trucks.
Gordon grumbled
as he pulled coaches.

One day,
a circus came
to town.

Now the engines
were even busier.

Henry pushed
the trucks.
Gordon pulled
the coaches.

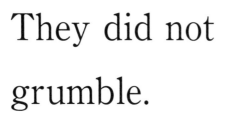

They did not
grumble.
Henry and Gordon
liked the circus.

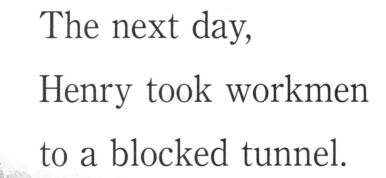

The next day,
Henry took workmen
to a blocked tunnel.

The workmen
picked up their tools.
"Time to clear the line."

They walked inside.

Something big was
in the tunnel.
It would not move.
It grunted.
It was alive!

They ran outside.

The Foreman had a plan.
Henry could push trucks
into the tunnel.

"Wheesh," said Henry.
Henry did not like
tunnels.
He was scared.

Henry pushed the
trucks.
They went
into the dark tunnel.
BUMP!

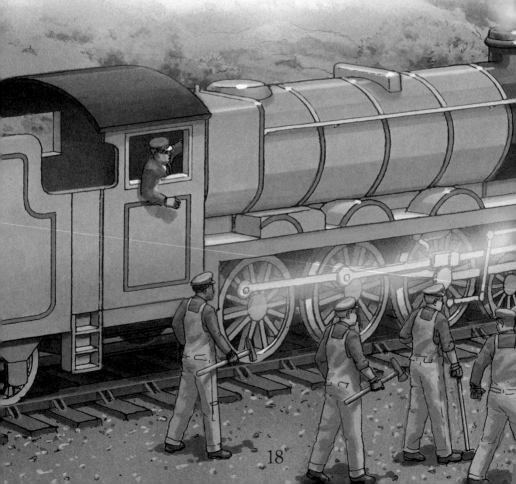

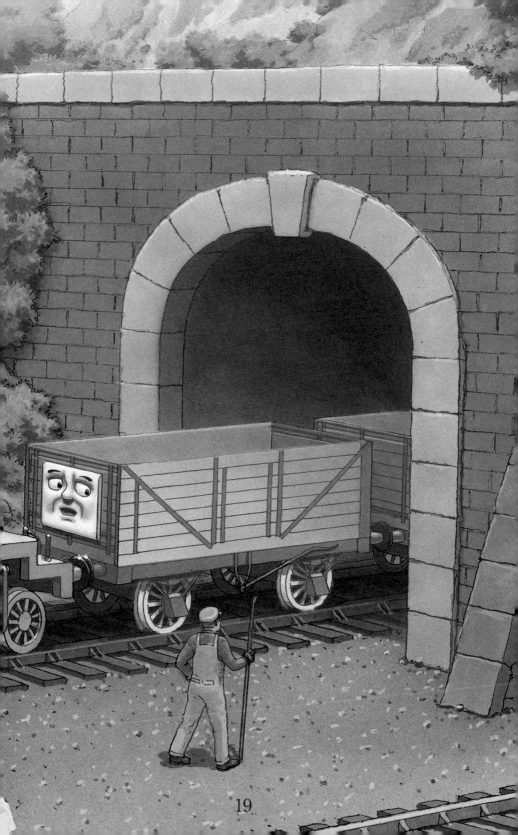

Henry pushed hard.
The big, scary thing
pushed back.

Henry pushed harder.
The big, scary thing
pushed hardest!
Henry inched
backwards.

First,
Henry was pushed
out of the tunnel.
Then the trucks
were pushed out.

At last,

they saw what

was in the tunnel.

It was an elephant!

And he looked cross.

He had run away

from the circus.

The workmen fed him
and gave him
lots of water.
The elephant felt better.

Henry felt better, too.

He let off steam.

Whoosh!

Henry's steam scared
the elephant.
Splash!
Poor Henry.

It was time to go home.
Everyone laughed
at Henry.

"An elephant
pushed me and
splashed me,"
Henry grumbled.

But in the Shed,
Henry told
his funny story.
His friends laughed.
This time
Henry laughed, too.